SPARK

A STORY AND POEMS LIT AFLAME

Excerpts from
STORM OF ROSES:
A Compilation of Poetry and Short Stories

E. TARA SCURRY

Chrysocolla Publishing
P.O. Box 4858
Silver Spring, MD 20914

Manufactured in the United States of America

With love,

And hope

To those who have been hurt.

Suffering does not have to be your life

Don't give up. Live to see the better days

*All battles are first won or lost,
in the mind.*

—Joan of Arc

CONTENTS

Introduction

As a storyteller, I'm always looking for more ways to make the world a better place through my stories. Publishing Storm of Roses in 2006 was my first attempt at making this happen. I'm beyond thrilled to release the 2nd Edition of Storm of Roses and get its first "single", SPARK into your hands!

I have always admired how musicians find creative ways to share their art with the world. Taking their lead, I hope you enjoy this taste of what Storm of Roses will offer. Rest assured there's much more where this came from!

Thank you for picking up your copy of SPARK: A Story and Poems Lit Aflame.

CHAPTER I

SPARK

SPARK
(DISCLAIMER: Violence, Miscarriage, Torture, Abuse, Cannibalism)

An abused girl's tipping point forces her
to seek revenge by telling disgusting lies...

He's drunk. There's no mistaking the off-beat clap of his worn boots against the dirt floor. Heavy-handed, foulmouthed, and bad-spirited, he's like all the men in our Turbid Orilon Lake commune. Endlessly vile.

Mother says Father's good spirit flew away when his first union dissolved. The priest gave him Beth. She died shortly after three stillborn babies fell out of her belly. Two boys and a girl. Mother says when she was given to Father, there was nothing she could do to compete with Beth's memory. Beth and Father's union was arranged as all are, but they had loved each other before the priest had put them together. When Beth died, all the good that was in him died too.

Tonight, Father could have passed out in the pub like last time, but no. Instead, the wooden door shivers against its hinges. The lake splashes a stone's throw outside our door. Startled awake, the water cows with their large dark-brown cyclops eyes groan, murmur and cry like exhausted babies desperate for sleep.

Mother squeezes my arm, her silent warning that I should pretend to sleep. Father is more likely to leave us alone if we ignore him. My little brother, Louis, curls up against Mother's side. We three have our own cots, but we prefer to push them together, away from Father's cot on the other side of the room.

Father mutters sharp, quick words. He's complaining about our cottage, looking for something. I hear a dull cascade as something falls. Probably wooden cups. Father snorts. I open my eyes. He is strong with ripples of solid muscle surrounded by his protruding belly. Mother's eyes are squeezed shut. I don't know how she manages to cry so hard without making a sound. Mother can do a lot of things I don't understand. She can endure the impossible. Live a lie.

"This place is disgusting."

It was perfectly clean before you started knocking things down. Mother cleaned every single bowl so you wouldn't beat her with them.

"Where is my food?"

You ate it before you went to the pub. What does it matter? If we don't do anything wrong, you just make it up.

I shift my eyes from my mother's face. The twin moons shine bright through a crack in our wooden walls. In a month, the moons will be full. I will be fifteen, and Louis will be eight, as we share a birthday. Mother always says that twin full moons on your birthday are a sign of the divine, bringing good luck.

Father destroys our fragile little kitchen. Throws himself against its walls. Shatters anything he can wrap his hands around.

Where does he get this energy from? He wakes up at dawn like the rest of us.

Silence.

Good. He passes out on the floor. We'll step over him in the morning. There will be no beatings tonight.

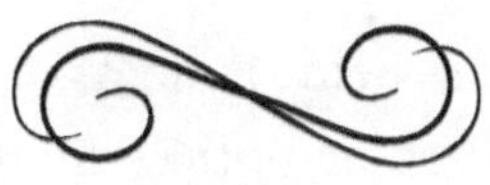

"Finish your porridge. Don't be here when he wakes." Mother waves her hands at us. "Get."

My lips tremble. "We don't want you here when he wakes, either," I say.

She holds our faces in her hands and shakes her head. Her eyes are red and tearing. "I'm so sorry. I know. I'll be all right."

"No, you won't," Louis whimpers.

Once she finishes her duties in the cottage, she'll go into the fields like the rest of us. If, that is, Father doesn't render her useless once he finally wakes.

"Besides," she adds, "I need to clean up my special powders." Her hair is thick and wiry, like a tangle of sharp bushes. Her hair pin sticks up like a thorn. One of her crooked teeth protrudes slightly out of her mouth as her lips tremble, but she is beautiful to me. Field soil dusts her coppery-brown skin, smooth and specked with barely visible freckles. "You mean your 'cooking spices'?" I say, brows raised. She's relentlessly secretive about the contents in her special jars.

She shakes her head. "Just go!" She snaps her fingers. She points toward the door, but her eyes tell us she wants another hug.

Louis and I take one last glance at our father's slumped-over frame, wrap our arms around our mother, then rush out the door.

The sun's heat immediately permeates my thin rags. I roll up my flimsy sleeves, and it bathes my skin. "Can I go to school today?" Louis tilts his head and raises his hand over his eyes.

"Go to school. I'll go to the field. If he asks, tell him you worked the field. Father never remembers or notices anything important anyway."

"Okay."

I wrap my arms around his slight frame and hand him a cloth filled with bread, apples and nuts.

"Don't forget. You're the one that has to go to school. When you're old enough, you'll get us out of here." I rub his bald head playfully. Mother recently shaved it when she discovered critters living there. "Remember the places far beyond the lake and mountains?" I ask. "Full towns of women and children who've found asylum. Freedom from the priests and their stupid unions. We're going to get there. We can make it."

"I know." He smiles for the first time all morning. His eyes are green just like mine, but his teeth are crooked like Mother's. I have Father's straight teeth and pale skin. Louis and Mother are brown like the murky lake that runs through our village.

I smile too. The reality of getting away from Father and Turbid Orilon Lake are the only things that could accomplish that feat. That and Richard.

I turn and run away, forcing the thought of Father out of my head. I stop walking as a smell jolts me, making my nose curl. I hate the fields. They reek of human flesh. The priests have too many laws and punishments, and their favorite is death by fire. Men and women burned bloody and black at the stake.

"Yah, I know. It's bad!" Richard shouts as I draw near. "Only fire can burn the Devil out of heretics." He laughs. His thick, long hair sits braided in a flat circle around his head, save for a stray bang that keeps touching his right eye. "Ever since that inquisitor was appointed, we've been getting burned at the stake breaks pretty much every week! One wrong breath and next thing you know, you're up in flames! Should I feel bad that I'm actually happy about it? The breaks from work, I mean."

I love the way the double suns glisten against his hay-colored skin. He's a few months older than me, but he likes when I take charge. He winks at me with his dark-brown eyes and shifts his gaze down to my stomach. I look past him at the deep ditch. The spotted water cows hear his laugher and take the opportunity to beg for food. Richard follows my gaze to the water cows and sprinkles dried hay across the water. They bellow in appreciation. When the water cows saunter out of the lake to sunbathe twice a day, we milk them and pull off the delicious large blue crabs that get tangled into their long matted manes.

"Don't be so loud about it! Best just not say or think anything about it at all." I wrap my dirt-stained faded-green rags tighter around my body with a wry smile. I'm getting noticeably bigger. It was Richard's way to make light of the terrible things that happen around us. To us.

Richard and I share the same type of pain: ruthless assaults from our fathers. Yet we still find joy in each other. Richard is the clearing in my storm. He feels the same about me too. I suppose we are a bit too happy together. I have been with child for many months now.

Richard nods, motions to my womb and reaches for my hand. "Not speaking about things doesn't make them disappear."

I want nothing more than to wrap myself in his arms and feel his strong weight holding me, comforting me. My heart longs for me to be held by him, but my feet force me to step back. Avoid his hand touching mine. I hate my life.

"What's wrong?"

"You want people to see us?" I scold him. "We have to be careful. *You know that*," I whisper, drenched in self-pity.

"I want to be with you! Get out of here. Your mother already knows." He looks at me sternly, pausing until I give him my full attention. "We can't let your father find out. He'll kill you. I'm not willing to let that happen."

I shake my head and hold back tears. "If Father wants to kill me, he will. No one can stop him. I can't leave Mother and Louis. Ever."

"That's my point," he says. His hand tremors. "We need to get out of here because once he knows, it's over. We can take your mother and brother with us. I'm surprised your mother took it so well."

I pick up my large basket and begin filling it with dry hay. "She's more afraid than upset. Keeps making me pray on my knees for forgiveness every chance she gets. She makes me snort some powder mixture. Says it will give me strength for what's to come, or something like that."

"Did you do it?"

"Yah. Of course."

"What is up with your mom and those powders?"

"I don't really know. Don't say anything. Next thing you know, she'll be burning on the stake."

I immediately regret my words. I trust Richard and don't want him to think otherwise. Plus, I feel guilty speaking about Mother that way. With my bad luck, my words will become a reality. Tonight before bed, I'll pray and replace my negative words with better ones.

"Come on, Diana, you know I wouldn't. Even if my mother were alive, I'd still like your mom better. *You know that*," he teases.

I nod and offer a smile. His father strangled his mother to death three years ago. Our commune leadership declared it was her fault. No woman deserved to live if she could not be obedient to her husband. He didn't get in trouble, but the priest didn't put a new wife on him, either.

"You're right. I know." I throw a handful of dry hay in his face. His eyes light up, and he grins.

"Come on!" I shout. "We have to finish the water cows, chickens and pigs."

"I love you. Whatever happens, I'll always be with you." He grabs my basket and covers our faces with it so others can't see if they look our way. I stand on my toes and kiss him.

I stare at the dirt floor with blurry eyes. I can't focus. Blood drips from my face. Is it my nose or my mouth? My stomach aches. Burning. Hurting.

"Who's been at you, Diana? I'm not going to ask again."

I try to answer Father, but sharp words catch jagged in my throat. I cough on my own blood, and my throat hurts from him choking me. I blacked out, but that didn't stop the pain. I can't see, but I can feel everything. I moan and keep shifting my legs. My whole body trembles.

My life slips away with every drop of blood that clots out of me. When I feel myself slip into the afterlife, I scream in my heart as I fall fast. My baby girl is pressed tightly against my chest; there is no way I'm letting go. Like a stone in a slingshot, something pulls me back before the air pushes out of me, like I have been kicked in the stomach. My baby slips through my fingers and continues to fall. I scream and whimper. Reaching out in vain for my child. I hang there, swinging gently back and forth. My baby falls into the darkness. I can't see her anymore. It's as if there is a thin string holding me between the two worlds, not letting go. The thinnest of threads with an unmatched strength that has been waiting for me. Ready to hold me. Refusing to release my soul into the darkness.

Mother sits with me, my head on her lap and my legs curled under me as she strokes my hair. At dawn, my mother's scream raised me from my bizarre revelations. I notice that a large puddle of blood developed under me and stained my pale legs.

"My heart burns." I cry. I can hardly hear my own words.

Father wakes, but he only stares at us. Mother shouts at Louis to go fetch Mrs. Anna, who is the midwife. Father leaves and drags Louis with him.

"Your girl-child has gone to Heaven," Mrs. Anna explains. "The Lord is merciful." She touches my hair gently.

I look away from Mrs. Anna to the tiny, bloody and limp baby in my arms. I hold her as long as my mother will let me. The baby has a birthmark over her eyebrow. She is so precious.

"He blessed you by granting your prayers. Took away what would have been an extra mouth to feed," she whispers confidently, patting me on the head.

I never prayed for that.

"Get some rest. Drink lots of water." She withdraws, nods to my mother and smiles at me before leaving. "You'll be all right."

"I want my baby," I whine with a groan, turning my head from left to right.

"You'll have more babies," Mother says gently.

"I don't want more. I want this one," I cry.

"Then pray. Take this," she says, opening her hand.

We pray together, then I snort every pinch of powder from her palm.

I sleep for a long while. When I wake, Mother is standing over me with a large bowl of soup.

"That smells great. Where's mine?" Louis asks. He peers into the bowl. "That looks like meat! We haven't had any in as long as I can remember."

"Sweetheart, this is a special soup just for your sister," Mother says as she lifts the spoon to my chapped lips. "To help her feel better." I accept the spoon and swallow the finely cut, tender chunks. I look past her to our small kitchen. Three of her special powders are open and sitting on the wooden counter. The smooth brown walls of our cottage are rotted and unstable, dark with patches of mold.

My eyes open wide. This was delicious.

"That's not fair," he says.

"I can share, Mother." My voice comes hoarse. "Who gave us meat? That was nice of them." My throat hurts, and the warm liquid is soothing against it. "Louis, come here."

"No!" Mother says sharply, shooing him away. She pauses and regains her composure, speaking gently, "This is Diana's. Louis, your supper is still warm. It's over there wrapped in the plantain leaves." She motions towards it. He obeys.

The cot is cold against my skin. I cover myself with a thin blanket and wring my hands. Clasp them so hard that it hurts. I pray—no, beg—God to make my father leave us alone. I rub my upper arms for comfort and hug my shoulders. I stop fighting the memories. Memories of dark ghosts in my father's form, yanking my hair and cursing me. Unable to speak or just muttering to myself, I want to die. I need the pain to end.

I'm overwhelmed with an insatiable itch that steals my hot tears, dissolving them into a dark cloud with grotesque red and black veins. A wicked, floating, vaporous threat full of blood and lightning that strikes and soaks me dripping wet. Shocked and steaming, my heart frazzled, soul scorched.

A voice vibrates against my ears as it crawls from dark corners, resting under my cot and singing from my pillow. A pleading voice that lets loose in the shadow of the moonlight. Rocking me awake with a ferocious melody. A harmonious tune of desperation, protection and survival.

Confusion hurls my mind in different directions. My heart grieves without peace, full to the rim with burnt ashes. I'm so angry I can hardly breathe.

Eventually, a realization burns my heart and pushes into my veins: the inevitable infinity song that has no end will continue to haunt me unless I submit and create the final notes myself.

This bright light of awareness surges through me from the grisly lightning cloud in Heaven's sky. I'm given a new heart, and it's like it's cut from the chest of the supreme God herself. I'm no longer frazzled and brutalized but starving and powerful.

There's a throbbing ache in my core—fiery heat. Finally, I bring forth my voice. My own dark song. A scream. I crave the feel of my baby in my arms. I want to smell her. Touch her. Kiss her little feet!

At dawn, Father drags me toward the door, forcing me off my feet. I collapse. I don't care what he's doing. It can never be worse than what he has already done.

"You always give me a hard time," he sighs, shaking his head. He blinks one eye, and sweat falls into it. His upper eyelid is droopy, nearly covering his whole eye. "What's your problem?"

"You," I sneered.

"Didn't you hear Dulcitius of Marburg?" His voice is sharp. "Everyone has their part. When you quit, it affects all of us. I can't stand when everyone complains about you."

"Really?" I scoff, throwing my head back. "I don't care what that inquisitor says. None of them care about us. They want us afraid. On our knees." I'm so drunk with disdain that my next words shoot out of my throat. Piercing the air like the cries of those at the stake as the first lick of the flames mauls their toes.

"You mean, when I quit, it affects *you*. We pick up *your* slack when you're drunk and can't work. Now you have to work like the rest of us." My eyes widen, and my fear sheds away like a snake's skin. A poisonous snake.

I push myself upright. "They don't complain about me; *you* complain to them about me. About all of us!" An irresistible urge to argue comes over me. "I know the truth. Your whole reality is a lie."

"You. Your mother. Both of you don't see what's around you. Barely enough of anything for anyone. Half-rotted crops. Witches and demons always trying to trick us." He waves his hand into the air. "Whatever we've done wrong, we need to fix it. With the help of Dulcitius of Marburg, we will. We must keep praying that God stops punishing us. She's already taken away my family. I don't need you, your mother and even Louis to mess up more than we already have. All of you just keep God's wrath on me. I can't take any more."

He clasps and unclasps his hands, shaking his head down at me.

"If God has already taken away your family, who are *we*?" I open my arms wide. A laugh curls out of my mouth and slaps him in the face.

He hits me. The blow knocks my eyes shut. Once I open them, I feel like I have poisonous venom. It oozes from my belly into my throat, boils over and shoots out through my eyes. If he would just look at me, I know my glare would kill him.

Father is like a worn-out rag doll, the kind we make with straw and mud from the lake. He has no words left, only slumped shoulders and unwilling eyes. Suddenly, he stalks out of the cottage, almost tripping over himself as if he couldn't get away from me fast enough. I know the painful ache of his blows will follow me for hours. The one on my face and the other deep in my heart. Being together as a family with Father would be impossible. I have always felt this way, but now I am certain.

I stumble back to my cot. I rest my cheek onto my pillow, careful not to bother the swollen side. I raise my hand to my face; its trembling. My pillow is singing to me again. It's an unsavory song but soothes my fear and commands me to change the path of my life.

As my pillow's song quiets, I imagine Mother and Louis far off tending the water cows. That is my job. I do need to get to work, regardless of what Father says. No more water cows, not now. There's a different job I must do. I wince when I hear the door slam.

"You whore!" Richard's father, Mr. Kempe, spits, glowering at me. His lips are curled, and droplets of sweat decorate his thick brows. I push myself off my cot and cower against the wall. There is nowhere to hide.

"I pulled your father off of Richard today. This is all because of you." He comes at me. "How dare you corrupt my son. I will send you to hell!"

My fear breaks into sharp pieces at my feet, and the heat in my veins bubbles over. I stare daggers into him. Tearing him to shreds with my eyes, daring him to come closer. There's no room for the self-pity of my past; it was sliced out and bled to death over an open flame. Only hunger, power and change can come into my nightmare. They will wake me up.

Finally, Mr. Kempe hits me. He wraps his hands around my neck; he's hurting me. I swing and punch blindly all around. My fists ache sharply each time they slam against his pudgy frame. I'm strong. I'm angry. I'm crazy. I'm going to kill him!

All of a sudden, he stops, and I'm still swinging. I can hardly see him. His weight lifts off of my cot, and I consider going after him. My knuckles ache, and I'm breathless, so I don't. My eyes swell, foggy with tears, but I see him now. With a distorted face and busted lip, he spits at me. He runs into the wooden meal table, stumbles back, then lunges forward out of the door. I'm so glad Richard is nothing like his father. As I am nothing like mine—at least, I don't think so. I remain the rest of the day in my bed, cheeks soaked with silent tears.

It's the strangest thing not to be able to speak with Richard. He was caught hanging around my cottage waiting for a chance to sneak in and see me. This is why Father and Mr. Kempe believe I have been with Richard to make my baby. I could hear Richard limping outside. Richard swore to them that he was concerned about me because of our friendship, but they knew better. Father forbade me to see him, and his father forbade him the same. Mother has taught me how to write a few things and play with small numbers, so it didn't stop me from scribbling a note to him. I wrote that I had a plan to change everything. To make things right. I wrote that he must destroy the note in the murky lake after reading it. A few weeks ago, someone was sent to the stake for protecting runaway heretics. Like Richard, I actually look forward to the executions. Everyone in our commune is given a break from our labor and made to watch.

With this in mind, I make my way to Dulcitius of Marburg's house. I should be frightened to confront him, but I'm more excited than anything else. Each step I take toward the inquisitor's house, my grin grows more wicked.

Every stone under my feet pinches me. My sandals are thin and worn. With each step, the dry brownish-green dirt kicks up and threatens my eyes. The heat of the two suns slowly cuts deep into my shoulders. I rub them gently. It's nothing compared to my life's horror—the life father thrust on us. I'm not afraid of these memories anymore. They'll give me the strength to change my life.

My eyes begin to ache, and I rub them. Despite the painful throb in my head, I see the sprinkle of slender, curvy trees with their naked branches marking my path. Fruit and leaves hardly last on our trees. We are all so desperate to pick every fruit and rip away any leaves in which to wrap around our food for steam cooking over fire pits.

Guards stop near the inquisitor's door, and I feel as pitiful and miserable as I ever have. A thick man with broad shoulders and filthy hair leers at me. His voice breaks as he speaks.

"What's wrong with you, little wench?" He grabs his groin and shakes his pockets. "Papa making you earn extra coins before letting you come home for supper?" He snickers at me. "I can help with that."

This guard doesn't have any teeth. I shake my head in denial and flinch at the sudden sound of rough footsteps coming near me.

"Dulcitius of Marburg isn't receiving anyone, girl." The second guard appears as he invades my personal space to stand in front of me; I instinctively take a few steps back.

I simply bore my eyes into both of them. I must look like a fool. Dirty blond knots for hair, teary green eyes, wearing a bucket of rags with sandals.

"He will receive me." My voice quivers. I walk past the toothless guard, but he grabs my shoulder. His hand rips open the sunburned skin there. I holler and tear myself away from his grip. I use the pain in my voice to make my declaration more believable. "He will see me. My father is a demon, and if I do not see Dulcitius, our whole village will be cursed!"

The second guard spits on the dirt and walks toward the entrance of the lair. The guard's eyes widen, then narrow. He turns around, and I follow him inside. I shiver, and I feel dizzy. I don't want to be anywhere near these two men. I'm not given a choice to sit, so I stand. Slow and heavy footsteps clank loud like the beaten copper bell in the middle of our village square.

I wipe sweat from my eyes with my flimsy sleeve as a cloaked figure comes toward me. The cloaked man is thin. His eyes are wrinkled and somber. Patches of dark curls pepper his balding head. He shouts as if I'm in another room instead of standing right before him. "Who is the heretic?"

"M...My father. He forces sin onto our family and worships the Devil every night."

The inquisitor looks at me warily. "Why only now is it that you confess this?"

I shoot back, "I am afraid! He has become more and more vicious. At first, he only conversed with demons. Now I believe he is becoming one!"

He motions for the guards to leave the room. I watch as he slithers onto a fancy stool, and his robe flows past his knees, completely covering his feet. "Tell me what you know. I'll have the three high priests preside over this case."

I tell him lies of my father's heresy, making sure to include Mr. Kempe's partnership in it all. His guards order me to lead them to my home. Father isn't there, so they follow me to the pub. People turn and stare at us as we walk together. They know death is coming. No sooner do I point out my father than they drag him, arms flailing and lungs wailing, to the town dungeon. Two of the guard's curse and take off in the direction of Mr. Kempe's cottage.

I stand and watch until I'm surrounded by silence. Father's broken sandals are strewn in the dirt. I explain in detail to Mother about the toothless guard because I'm particularly afraid of him. She kisses my forehead, holding me in her comforting arms. She tells Louis that I am the blessing we have been praying for.

"Something sparked in you, Diana. You're letting it change you. Take you over," Mother said.

I shake my head. My lips narrow, and the corners of my mouth turn downward. Dulcitius of Marburg sent his servants to notify the commune that we are to meet in the courtyard in the morning. We all will be required to watch the trial. For some reason, I assumed Father would be burned at the stake, which always happens in the field. When they tell us to meet at the courtyard, that usually means they're going to torture the accused on the large wooden stage or boil them alive in an oversized cauldron.

"Why are they taking Father to the courtyard instead of the field?" I ask.

Mother pauses in thought before putting away the last of our wooden bowls on a shelf. "I think because he's being tried for more than just heresy. You said he raped, murdered and spoke with demons, right?"

"I can stop this. Tell them I don't remember anything anymore."

Mother bites her lip and shakes her head, her breath quickening. "Why? You feel sorry for your father? Have you finally found some love in your heart for him?"

"I always had love for him." I pause and correct myself. "I always had hope. You know, that he could love us back. At least not hate us. That things could be different."

I glance to Mother, then to Louis who is resting on his cot, carving a water cow out of a piece of wood.

Mother shakes her head. Her hands are busy cleaning the cottage. She stops and looks right at me as her rag falls to the floor. "Don't fight it," she says, her hands trembling. "Don't push down your anger. Your pain. Don't be like me." Her voice strains. "Don't you see where it got me? I can't get away from him. What type of a mother am I?" She twitches, and I can tell she is fighting back tears. "I can't protect my own children."

I don't remember ever seeing her so wretched.

"My greatest fear is that you and Louis will see what a dull coward I am. Hate me for what I've done. What I couldn't do." She wipes her brow and lets her tears fall.

"Your father got dealt a losing hand. I was put onto him." She nods, then pauses, wipes her sleeve across her face. "Uglier and more senseless than his first wife."

I open my mouth to speak, but she holds up her hand, silencing me. She shouldn't talk about herself like this. None of this is her fault. A wife has no protection against a husband's will.

"If he had gotten a better deal, he would have been a better man. A better father. He's not a bad person."

"Not a bad person?" I break in. "You know what he's done. To all of us. To my baby." My voice trails, and heat rises from my core.

"When bad things happen to good people, they can change," Mother says, her voice higher pitched. "I saw that in your father's eyes. I see it in you, now."

"What does that mean? I don't understand what you want me to do."

"I'm not going to make your decisions. You are strong."

"No, I'm not."

"But you are. You can be." Her tears stop, and she meets my gaze. She pushes a frizzy lock of hair behind her ear. "I can't fix my mistakes. I'll be damned, though, if I watch you make the same."

She comes toward me and opens her arms. I fall into them. I need her. Despite everything, I never doubt my mother's love for me. I am never sure, though, if she loves herself.

"I want you to do better than me. Be better," she whispers and kisses the top of my head. "Don't you ever let anyone put out that spark in you. Control you." She squeezes me and gives me a shake. "Do anything but be like me."

She holds me away and tilts my head up with the palm of her hand. "All I know is fear and love. Fear of everything and love for you and your brother." She wipes a tear from my eyes with her thumb. I didn't realize I was crying.

"You've got to know more than me! Know some courage. Know some faith." She pauses, then says coldly, "To know when to stop feeling sorry for those who don't deserve it."

Clad in a short black robe that falls to the tops of his knees, one of the executioners, Mr. Tackie, strips Father naked and dry-shaves him. Says it makes discovering the Devil's mark less tedious. When not torturing and executing people, Mr. Tackie fixes boots and shoes next door to the blacksmith.

The weight of the stares makes me tremble. I'm supposed to speak. In a ferocious storm of tears and determination, I explain what my father and Mr. Kempe have "done." The other executioners are eager to get their hands on him. I can't speak fast enough. They quickly wave me away and prick Father with the thick, blunt needle of a bodkin. His shoulders look dislocated, probably from having them pulled up behind his back. His hip joint is forced from its socket. We watch as Mr. Kempe's toenails are torn out with turcas. We are careful not to show too much compassion lest someone think we sympathize with Devil worshipers. Father's one eye is gouged out, while the other is burned out of its socket. His front teeth extracted with pliers. He spits onto the floor every time the raw sockets fill with blood.

I stand close to Richard as we look across the crowd of people from the high stage, then shift our gazes back to look at Mr. Kempe slumped over next to Father. Mother is in the back somewhere with Louis. I can't see her. She doesn't want to watch, but everyone is required to be present during these punishments.

I look at Richard's hand, and I want to hold it—but I can't. Not yet. Richard has wrapped his arms around himself as if it can stop him from shaking. He keeps his head down so he doesn't have to see his father suffering. It doesn't matter. All of us can still hear it. There is no escape.

I notice Mr. Kempe's blotched and red skin from when he was forced to take a scalding hot bath laced with lime, which sears the flesh. The priest gets our attention and makes sure we watch as Mr. Kempe's right foot is covered with lard and roasted slowly over the fire until his bones crack and pop as the marrow drips onto the flames.

"Is that all you have left to say?"

I look each priest in the eye. One is tall, one fat, and the other so short his feet don't touch the ground as he sits. They wear robes and strange pointed hats.

"Yes. It's the same as before, your grace. My Father worships the Devil."

I pause, and they watch me, clearly waiting for more information.

"He told me the demons said he must commit sins against God in order to win their favor. To be a head Devil priest, he had to commit sin by incest. Father raped me." I know it is a lie, but in my heart, it's true. The tears start to come again. My reliable, grief-stricken tears.

"He would kill me if I told," I say. "But I trust God. I know the Lord. She will protect me for speaking the truth."

I shift from one foot to the other. "When he found out I was pregnant, he beat me in hopes of killing the child so there'd be no evidence. A few days after that, he sent Mr. Kempe into our cottage to break the law of union and morality by raping me too. That the sin would please the Devil!"

"Yes," the heavy-looking priest says. He leans to the side, and the chair creaks. I can't understand how it continues to hold his weight.

"The witness, your neighbor, said she saw Mr. Kempe come into your house on the same day you said."

"Yes, your grace." I wipe sweat from my face. The suns bite at me with their rays. We have been out here all morning. Father gets silenced each time he offers an explanation. He denies wrongdoing, and they continue to torment him with questions and pain.

"And you, boy," the same priest says. "Do you have anything else to add?"

Richard shifts his weight from one foot to the other, then shakes his head, silent.

What does it matter? The servants are already bringing in a large bowl filled with rats. The priests are going to torture them regardless of anything else we say. They mean to turn the bowl onto their bare stomachs and light a fire over the top. I've seen this once before. The rats panic and burrow into their bowels. It would take a while for Father and Mr. Kempe to die from the rats, but they would feel the pain immediately.

The dry, rotted stage creaks again as I glance at my feet. My slippers are blood-stained, the soles soaked. My nose keeps curling at the stench. I'm not sure if Father or Mr. Kempe soiled themselves or if it's the stink of their insides connecting with the air.

"So he tried to put the blame on you. That you impregnated the girl?" the tall priest asks Richard.

"She and I are friends," Richard mumbles. "We would never think about sinning." His voice cracks, and he wrings his hands. "We're not married. Too young to know of these things you're talking about."

Richard and I return to our work tending the water cows. The church takes a little of the money my father had. Father's debtors are too afraid to acknowledge any relationship with him, so we are permitted to keep the rest. Everything else we had didn't mean anything. I scan our small cottage: flimsy cots, tattered towels and dented wooden cups.

Mother is filling a bag with her spices by wrapping the delicate containers with the cushion of our raggedy clothes.

"What's going on?" I ask, but I already know.

"In the last few months, I've been praying and sprinkling blessings," she says without looking at me. "But it's not safe. Never will be. In Turbid Orilon Lake, everyone will burn to their death. By fire or by sorrow."

I nod, pick up an empty potato sack and start shoving my clothes into it.

"Your father had it coming. If we stay here, we will too. It will be our fault."

She shakes her head. "When I prayed, the holy spirits told me that the priests will never let you marry Richard. They said they're going to marry you to the toothless guard in the spring. I'll end up someone's third wife. Louis will be an unwanted stepchild. There's nothing good for us here."

The thought of being the toothless guard's wife causes my limbs to tense. "Absolutely, never ever!"

Mother nods in agreement, and Louis raises his head as if to check if I'm all right.

"Louis hasn't finished his education yet. How can we take care of ourselves?" I ask.

"I don't know," she says, opening and closing her hands in frustration. "All I know is the holy spirits say we aren't safe. We've got to leave immediately. We listen to God, and she will take care of the rest."

"Are we going to the towns beyond the lake and mountains? I don't want to raise my child here." I place my hand over my belly.

"Your child?" Her largest crooked tooth pokes out as she smiles.

When my daughter is placed in my arms, my mouth falls open and I squeal. It feels good to have my husband, Richard, at my side and our daughter in my arms. I never regret my past, what I did. I embraced my time for revenge and lied with a confident heart. Yet God found it in her heart to have mercy on me.

"She's back!" I shout, squeezing my eyes shut and opening them again.

I have seen her face before! I know my baby. The exact same little eyes and nose. The same birthmark over her eyebrow. My girl-child did not go to Heaven. Her spirit left the old body, yes—but stayed with me, only to return right back in my womb. All is finally well.

I take in a deep, satisfying breath and nod to my beloved Richard. He rubs my back and kisses my cheek. My mother hums faintly as she pours warm stew into a wooden bowl for me. It is hearty with beans, corn and barley. I watch Louis play with a soft toy made of braided hay in the corner of the room. A few days earlier, we celebrated my birthday along with his tenth one. We have found a new commune beyond the lake and mountains where we were welcomed with open arms. They helped us build two cottages side by side. Mother took up work as a medicine woman and healer, so we are able to get by while Louis goes to go to school every day. Richard and I quickly found ourselves working alongside the water cows, like old times but better. Water cows are such large and gentle creatures, but if you don't feed, water and pet them enough, they will bite your ankles and drag you drowning into the water. Most are too afraid to tend them, but Richard and I can't get enough of them.

A warm, soothing sensation takes hold of me. Is this what peace feels like? I shift my gaze back to the child in my arms. I hold her close, lean down and inhale. She smells like an enchanting angel. Her scent does something powerful to me. She smells the way beauty and purity might if they could be laid into a barrel and churned with a plunger, like how we whip milk to make butter. I touch the fine hair of her head. I run my knuckles along her delicate cheeks. I kiss her little feet.

The End.

CHAPTER
II

POEMS

The Essence of God

The image of God
is
The uniting of man and woman
Why do we call Him "he"?

You are masculine and feminine
You have a child
You are the *holy family*
The Father, the Son Jesus, and the Mother Spirit

The Father does not spare us his commands, anger, and punishment
The Son is our friend, speaking and walking with us
The Mother lays her hands on our flesh and gives peace to our souls

The Father
Jehovah
Gives us the rules of his house
He explains and is clear, we
often wish to discount those rules most difficult
especially about tithing and fornication
But there are no excuses for disobedience
He answers our questions with truth and provides for our needs
He is strong, powerful, and jealous
He demands respect and constant praise
He is a warrior, he is a protector
He is King
The Father has a vision of the big picture

He desires to give what is best for you to have
He says "No," "Yes," and "Not now" out of love
If you rebel, you regret

The Son
Jesus
Is our friend
He tells us when we are wrong, when we smell, and when
We are dirty
He is pleased with complete honesty
When we are not honest with our symptoms and sins
He knows his advice will mean nothing and withholds
Until we confess
Jesus hears our daily prayers and testifies to the Lord
When you stray from the Father's house
The Mother sends the Son to go fetch you
Jesus is hurt when you leave his side,
He is your friend who misses and worries about you
He gives you one hundred, then asks for ten back
So that he may give you two hundred, then ask for twenty
When you fight with him, he is the first to forgive
He is your conscience, keeping you from temptation and sin
He does not want you punished
by the Father's rod or drenched in the Mother's tears
Your best friend died so that you may live
He sacrificed his life, suffered false witness and torture
So that you may truly know what true friendship is

The Mother
Grace
Comforts and gives encouragement when we are weak
When our strength is dead
The Mother never gives up on her children
She is the epitome of forgiveness

The Mother monitors us as we sleep, eat, and play
Nurses us when we are sick or when our flesh is fading with illness
She patches us up when we hurt ourselves
Scolds us when we hurt others, compelling us to apologize or
forgive and
To "say it like we mean it"
The Mother coaxed you back into the Father's house
when Jesus brought you to His door
when you rebelled and were reluctant with shame
Come back home, child ... your Father will forgive you,
He will punish you, because We love you,
He will teach you the way, so you don't stray,
Come now, I can love you no more and no less,
She is God's Grace, affirming and giving
She praises us, spoiling us with Blessings we never deserve

Ode to Satan: The God of This Age

Bold and fiery dragon
Accuser of the brethren
Evil one
Tempter
All these you are
Only the ignorant and those apathetic to truth
Know you as Lucifer, that prosperous mistranslated myth

All things were created by God
You are a spirit, not a thing and physical
God saw everything he created; it was good
You are the epitome of evil
God created the heavens and the earth
The Word does not say God
Created the heavens, the earth, and hell
I will not believe what the Word does not say
I will not infer, assume, or add

But you, King of Demons
Powerful and heavy on our backs
Make mothers murder their babies
Fathers kill themselves from the inside out
Children bludgeon children

Only you
Are given such rein and authority
To dare go against the desires of God
To his very face
You have been in his mighty presence
How bold you are!

Impressive lying wonders and gifts the
Flesh truly appreciate
When we ask of you, immediately you answer
When I ask for your sweet wicked delights
Unlike the Lord, you never refuse me
You embrace and answer my prayers for the present
You never make me wait for your aid
You are on a timetable; God is not

Who are you, Satan?
God did not create you or hell
He does not mention your origin
But fills pages only on how to resist you, as if
Knowing that is more important than knowing your birth
Or the origin of hell since he
Created only the heavens and earth

Are you the personification of sin and wickedness
Or are you truly a spiritual entity?
I believe
You are a powerful, bold, and feeling spiritual being
For the Devil led Jesus to a high place to tempt him with
The kingdoms of the world
Sin did not lead Jesus
The Devil led Jesus to Jerusalem
Wickedness did not lead Jesus

God loves me, sin after sin
Despite my sins
You embrace me, sin after sin
Because of my sins

God created us as sinners from the womb
With you, I can be myself, as I was born to be
A sinner from the womb
You take me as I am
I am always welcome and greeted with enthusiasm

God makes me change before
I am welcome in his palace
I must take off my shoes
Clean my flesh and
Brush up my faith
With you
I can come as I am

Candle Love Spell

You will come back to me; my hand is in the magical air
You cannot resist your five senses
The elements will pull you to me
Like rain to the flowers of the earth
You will water my desires
You are pure, wet, and weak now
Fall from the clouds of my candle's smoke
I'll drink you forever

Mold you to my pleasure
You'll chase after me like
The light is destined to chase the night
You'll stick to me like
The scent of a flower

Rose quartz stones
Candles of red, white, and pink
The shadow of my obsession
Forces you to realize now
Because my hands are in the magical air
You're engraved toward your destiny
Don't fight, just come
My candle's light will guide you
Through the dark and confusion's reflections
Be comfortable on your knees
I won't let them bruise

On a soft fur carpet you will kneel
But kneel you shall

I love you with a terrible love
You've been bewitched by elements' mercy
My hands are in the magical air
You're engraved toward your destiny
You'll be he who stares with obsession
Eyes glazed over with incomprehensible love
It is I who shall smile and know how we came to be
It is I who shall smile and know why you can never be free of me
My intentions are pure and true
That I'll be forever with you
No one is better for you than me
I'm doing you a favor by enslaving you
Chains of love, cages of love
And you, my love
Are engraved toward your destiny
Stop fighting, just come
The light of my candle will guide you
Through the dark and confusions' reflections
Be comfortable on your knees
I won't let them to bruise
On a soft fur carpet you'll kneel
But kneel you shall

I love you with a terrible love
My intentions are pure and true
That I'll be forever with you
I am the only one who
Truly loves you

Doll

I was thrown
Tossed to the side
Glass eyes

I was used
Now I'm lost
Among his other dolls
In my little dress

He could have put me
Back on the shelf neatly
But I was cast back
I'm not even sitting straight
With my legs twisted,
My arm curled under me,
Head hanging to the side
I hate the way I look like this
Lifeless, deprived, worn

It's obvious to me
I am his doll
I was played with
I am old
He has a new doll
She's young and beautiful
Her dress isn't ragged like mine
I am of the old trend

I am an old toy
My parts creak
I kiss dust
Instead of his lips

As the days go by
I'm even less desirable
Dress turning gray
Dirt in my hair
And he doesn't even care
Why would he or anyone
Ever want to pick me up again?

I am a doll
Just a toy, turned off
My time is over, batteries dead
Expiration date, here
Now

No one will ever touch my hair again
No one will ever make me dance
No one will ever kiss my cheek as he
I am not alone, but I am by myself
On this shelf, away from his heart

My Castle Is Built

I do as I please
Say I can't
If it's good for me
I will
I will be mistaken
Get over it

My future is in my hands
Dig my own grave
Build my own castle
I will be mistaken
You say, an overachiever
I'd rather have a castle
Where one end is unseen from the other
Than a shack where
One must wipe her feet before going
Outside

Don't waste your time
Lashing vicious names with jealousy's tongue
You're already behind
Fate grabs at your ugly ankles
Swollen from standing in place
Fat with fake gratification

Tame me, my aspirations?
I will drink my fill of opportunities

Call me a shrew
But I've got an
Education
And hips

Whipping your own back
Standing in place
Trying to divert me
You remain still
Other times
You're foolish enough to run backwards
Tripping over yourself because you can't see
While I move on to important things

So keep digging your hole
Until it's dark and cold
Until the sand falls around and over you
Until you suffocate in your foolishness and die by yourself

Such a Pitiful Pebble Pushed

In bloom I'll grow
Then no more will your lies
Continue to molest my insides
I have no more worries

You're like the pebble that's been displaced
By the rough wind's sour breath
It was the ultimate sin to hurt me
You'll reap your own viciousness
I swear it

Such a pitiful pebble pushed
Along the cold waters of my lake
Forced over and wet with my sobbing
Down the waterfall, the pebble cracks
Like my smile when I see you bleed

Women of the Sky

Sky Cotton
Cloud
Pale white
Floats above in her bloated dress
Pregnant
Swollen round breast ready to pour
Rain
Smooth face like porcelain
Translucent eyes and colorless hair
Cotton suspended in air
Puff

Madame Lightning
She flashes her swords
Dress of sparkling light clinging to her hips
None dare kiss her lips

Luminary Sphere
Drenching earth with her scorching smile
Eyes able to burn through darkness
Round full-figured curves
A beauty which melts hearts
Turns eyes into ash
Orb of the daystar

Earth

The earth is alive
Her heart is the heated core
Skin, cool soil
Grass, the thin hair of her arms

We are the microorganisms
Sometimes we do right by her
Other times we don't
And she flushes us away in floods
Warps us with disease
Or rips us apart with hurricanes
Her antibiotics
Destroying us all, good and bad

Like bacteria
We've found ways to adapt
To flee and protect ourselves
We sicken her then
Poison her veins with our waste
Gorge ourselves fat with her blood
Like vicious powerful parasites

Unnatural Disaster

Woe it was unto the innocent and poor
Gigantic underwater earthquake drowning
Babies, tearing husbands from wives
Brothers and sisters and relatives never to set eyes
On one another until the next life

What a clever idea it was, blame it on Gaia,
Blame it on the Lord
It is man who is not blameless
Using their weapons under the seas,
Killing for their own purpose, hundreds of thousands
In about twelve disparate nations!

What a clever idea it was, blame lack of technology
Lack of monitoring, lack of notification systems
Who has heard of "lack of technology" in this age?
In an area prone to these storms of death of the past
Man didn't want to save lives that day

What a clever idea it was, leveling the pitiable beachfront
Sweeping away the poor, creating sympathy
Making room for the privileged to lay their nests of riches
Yes, so that money pours into the hands of man
Already prepared to receive it, so strategically placed they were
That they may plant their seeds of business without resistance
Under the guise of relief

Let a sociologist write a headline
Let the world step above and look back at itself
Without logs and dust in their eyes
Without their hands tied behind them, on
Their knees worshiping money they don't have
Praying shamelessly for self-interest and pleasure

Man thinks he is clever, but he is foolish
Justice is not ripe and grows on a tree in Eden
The hour it descends, the Son too shall fall from the clouds

Pray for the foolish man
Pray for the innocent and poor
Their souls snatched from the rural shores

A Comfort Woman's Testimony

I am sick and heated
The ceiling a blur before me
Yes, the numbness of my body is a blessing
But who is this that gives me mercy?
Since I know no god exists anymore
Because she's left me

She ignores my tears
As they seep into her bosom and disappear with my faith
She does not hold me nor protect me
She does not love me
And every other moment it is a different evil man
With the same full and evil swords
By which they bleed me
And drown my dignity and strength

I weep before they even look at me
I weep before they even beat at my head
I weep when I hear even the faintest sounds
Of their terrible murmurs and laughs

I cannot escape this tragic routine
Look, my legs are numb
They do not move, they cannot run
The doors and windows are guarded

They do not open for me, no light comes through
So here I lie
Hardly alone and hardly alive
My spirit is dead
Yet I survive
Or rather I am merely existing
As the evil man's pleasure
During the evil man's war

Algebra is Evil

All this confusion is feeding off my patience
Leave, I don't mind being the only one who sees wild things
misplaced
Giving my soul to it, day into the night; still no understanding
Eventually it'll be clear, not like a crystal; like a pencil in water it is
not what it seems
But it's taking too long, numbers within themselves, this is
ridiculous
Relieve me of this; it has no use to my aspirations; I do not need
to know this
Always on my mind, I must pass to continue, such useless madness
Idiot? No, I'm not. I just don't like it. I hate it. Pointless problem
solving
Someone get me out of this class; this is the last place I want to be
Enough of this nonsense; letters and numbers don't mix, like water
and oil
Violently, let us destroy and break this cycle of evil; I'm through
with it
Illuminating the need of its destruction and its obvious evil; let's
strike
Lastly, deliver me from its lingering evils, Shepherd. May I never
see it again!

Alone

I don't understand this plan
All I know is I'm alone
By myself, empty
With no one to touch my skin
How do I know I'm alive?
No one to hold my hand as I die

Screwed Over In The Dark

Floating on the boat of despair
The river of tears sending me forth
Eyes stinging from cold fear

Will you always be there for me
Or did you speak false seduction
For your own wicked amusement?

So that I may lie trusting beside you
Heart and body naked before those eyes
For you to break and take at your will

I'm sad and surprised
I thought you really loved me
Then why did you hold me,
Look deep into my eyes, and tell me lies?

I have passion in my pain
All this love-wishing was in vain
I don't want to spend a lifetime looking for someone
But you just had me, then left
For more fun

I have no love, no hope left, and no heart
You left it bleeding,
Still beating in the dark

The Circle

More meat means more meat to sell
Stuff the animals with growth hormones
Like brown stuffing in a dead turkey
Bloated, juice dripping down the side

I eat them animals and get fat
I eat them animals and get sick
Maybe I'll staple my stomach
Maybe I'll eat less
Okay, I ate less, but I'm still fat because
I'm still eating growth hormones
No one wins except them meat and diet industries

Meatier cows means more meat to sell
A fatter me means I eat more
So I buy me more meat
I might buy a gym membership
I buy more diet food, I have more hospital bills
Since I eat meat, I'm much more likely to get
Breast, colon, and prostate cancer, arthritis, stroke
High blood pressure and veins in my legs
My chances of getting that are higher than those
Strange vegetarian folks
Eating their funny food, drinking their 100% juice and anti-milk
They must know something I don't, to deprive themselves of real
food
Kinda like them religious folks, trying to be perfect

Maybe they know something I don't, to deprive themselves of the good life

I know that some farmers put in tranquilizers
To keep the animals calm, but I don't mind that
I eat the meat and tranquilizers be good for my own nerves
They put antibiotics in them too, that's good for me
I get free medicine every time I eat me some chicken or steak
So what if it makes me more resistant to penicillin
If I already have free medicine, I don't need penicillin

Over a lifetime, we eat about 750 chickens and turkeys
About thirty-six pigs
Meat got protein, lots of protein
They say it takes more energy to digest meat than we get from eating it
That our digestive organs wear down because of it, causing all sorts of stuff
Meat has a lot of fat, but I like my meat and milk
A car cost less than a hamburger, per pound
Eating meat might not be good for the planet, because of the industry
It messes up the water, air, and soil and takes ten times more energy than
It takes to satisfy them vegetarian eaters
If everybody like me reduced animal eating by 10%
The hungry of the world could be fed, because of the grain saved

It's not the nicest thing to do, to overcrowd animals in the stockyards
But I don't see it, so it's all right with me
It's not like they're *real* animals, like cats, dogs, horses, and bunnies
Those are nice, friendly animals
Chickens, cows, and hogs don't count

I don't see baby cows chained to dark pens so small they can't sit
Taken at birth to be slaughtered as veal, never to see light
I don't see live animals dangling from the ceilings, blood swelling
their faces
I don't see castration with scorching heat
With no pain relief, so they don't mate

It's cheap to stick a long rod through their anus to their mouth
until they die or
Stun them with electricity, slitting their throats to preserve the carcass
Decapitation, scorching and drowning them alive in boiling water to
Soften their skin for picking feathers and tender meat
I know it happens, it's true, but I don't see it so it's all right
Many times them chickens are starving and anxious, they try to eat
or peck each other
So their beaks are seared off without anesthesia
Chickens should know better than to pick at each other like that

Slaughterhouses violate more laws than any other type of business
Not just in the treatment but in the chemicals they inject
Raw meat covered in goo and blood, nasty
But once it's cooked with a little parsley on the side, it's delicious
I don't want to think about what it really is, who does?
Why do 30% of pigs die of heart attacks before being sliced open?
Maybe they understand the cries of those before them on the
butcher line
Maybe they're literally scared to death
But they aren't *real* animals
They don't have feelings and personalities like cats and dogs

Me and everyone else grew up on meat and I won't let it go
So don't try, don't waste your time
I don't want fake soy meat, tofu, or imitation meatloaf
I've never had it before, but I'm sure it's awful

The meat I eat isn't gross; it's delicious and juicy
I love the taste of dead castrated animal injected with chemicals
I can't pronounce

Cows and chickens are anxious, depressed, and scared
They breathe the aroma of torture and feel death inevitable
In the dirty dark stench, under the vile shadows of their pens
They produce anxious, depressed, and scared chemicals inside
I eat their anxious, depressed, and scared flesh
And now I must take more calm or happy pills
I'm not ignorant of why I am anxious and depressed
I know that causes it, but that's what my pills are for

I butcher and slice up billions of innocent, feeling animals
So what if it comes back to me; I get killed prematurely too
Breast, colon, and prostate cancer, arthritis, stroke
High blood pressure, heart disease
It's the circle of life
It's the circle of death
That's the way it is and I'm going to eat my meat
I'm going to pollute my earth
I'm going to eat more so the other half of the world starves
God didn't create animals as precious beings
God gave me permission to eat them
Otherwise He wouldn't have made them out of meat (But am
I meat? Doesn't count!)
So what if eating them means they get abused in the process
It's my right and I can't do anything about it
Nothing I want to do
When He said I have dominion over them, He meant
I can torture, impale, electrocute, beat, and break their bones
And mutilate their little squealing bodies
As it pleases me to do so that I may eat and grow fat
That was His purpose; I'm just being obedient

I'm too weak to stop eating meat; I like it
It tastes good
That organic milk is made by hand-milked and grain-eating cows
But the regular milk is made by machine-milked and
Dead-ground-up-cow-eating cows
Machine milking causes irritation, pus and blood get mixed into the
milk
I don't know what it would taste like without it, so I can't
Tell the difference, especially with the flavoring chemicals to mask
it, so what
Your nipples would probably get sore, bleed, and ooze pus if
You had a metal machine milking at them for twenty hours
nonstop too
That's why it stinks so bad when it gets a little old
And soy anti-milk lasts like five plus times as long in the fridge

Don't matter
I have dominion over women, children, and all animals of the earth
It's fair and it is my divine right
And I'm going to suffer
Just like the animals do when they die
It's the circle
I hurt them and they hurt me
I torture, murder, and castrate them and they
make me fat and give me heart disease!
It's the circle
It's fair

And in our separate ways
We're both too weak to stop it

Dangerous Baby Girl

You torture me, baby girl
Come closer, so precious
Would you like some sweets
For my sweet, precious baby girl?
You know I'm wrong
And dangerous
But so are you

Your mother dresses you in hot pants
That short skirt
I see your creamy small legs
So young and soft
Unmarred so far
Flat-chested and tiny all over
You torture me, baby girl
Your mother dresses you in tiny tank tops
Baby flip-flops
Pink skirt; I see your tummy

I've got to have your everything
Stay sweet and silent
Like a baby blueberry in a bush
Picked and squeezed of your innocence
Drenching my fingers in your sweetness
All over my hand

I see you looking at me
You love my attention
Your mother always lets me in
Let me buy you dolls and things
Beautiful, why would I lie?
So exposed and innocently sparsely clothed
You torture me
In your flower print tiny shorts
A single strap hanging from your shoulder
Hardly nine years old
You're dangerous, baby girl

Your mommy told you about men like me
You know it's not right
But she dressed you in hot pants
And you love my attention

You drew the cutest picture the other day
I was in your house
Your own father disregarded it
Your mommy hung it up on the fridge
But I told you it was marvelous!
What a talented Picasso you are!
Who's Picasso? The best and most creative artist
Who has ever lived!
And you, my sweet
You are the best I've ever seen!
I know you liked that,
Didn't you
You ate it up and kissed my cheek
You hate to see me go
And I'll keep it that way

I'll hurt you a little bit
But it's not my intention
But just indulge me for a few minutes
A few long heated minutes
You're so beautiful, the most precious thing
I've ever seen
In your dangerous hot pants
And pink thin tank top
Your mommy must dress you up like that
Just for me

Lavender

Lavender is my favorite color
Lavender like lilacs
Lavender like the flowers that cover my green garden
Smooth and silky petals
I like the velvety shade of lavender as the sun sets
And falls asleep in a rainbow at my windowsill
A baby purple, faint, shallow, and never deep; an immature violet
Looking as good as you smell
Feathery, warm, peaceful
Lavender …

Note to Readers

Dear Reader,

I hope you enjoyed SPARK: A Story and Poems Lit Aflame. I'm so grateful for your eyes on these pages! I deeply appreciate your support. The top three things you can do to support me are:

1. Write a Review. This is by far the most helpful and supportive thing you can do. Amazon, Goodreads, and Barnes & Noble are great places to start!

2. Subscribe to my blog and comment on my posts at https://etarascurry.com/blog/. There are also free stories and poetry on my blog that you can enjoy

3. Join my VIP List! by signing up through my website, https://etarascurry.com/. You'll receive freebies, special offers, free books, updates on my latest stories, and my quarterly *Apatite Books & Café Newsletter*

Thank you for reading and I welcome your feedback. Write to me at etarascurry@gmail.com or Chrysocolla Publishing P.O. Box 4858 Silver Spring, MD 20914.

You're also invited to hang out with me and like-minded friends on Twitter @ETaraScurry and in my Facebook Group: https://www.facebook.com/groups/etarascurry/

Having readers like you is my dream come true. I appreciate you! Stay in touch.

~ E. Tara Scurry

Also by E. Tara Scurry

STORM OF ROSES:
A Compilation of Poetry and Short Stories, 2nd Ed

Release Date: 2021

SYNOPSIS
Originally published in 2006, Storm of Roses, winner of the Best Books National Book Award in Poetry and an award-winning finalist in the "Indie Excellence 2007" Book Awards in the Poetry category, has been updated to incorporate revisions of short stories and poems, making it an even more tantalizing collection of literary art.

With bold musings about pleasure, pain, life, death, anger, spirituality, nature, compassion, fantasies and daydreams, this compilation is a provoking celebration of wisdom.

Within these pages, E. Tara Scurry delivers an intense and enchanting debut assortment of over 90 poems and 11 short stories initially written when she was between 7 and 23 years old.

A unique take at poetry and story-telling, Storm of Roses fluctuates convincingly from dark to sunny and violent to serene. Exceptionally captivating, it's a gathering of pieces for the tenacious and resilient.

CRACK OF DAWN
(The Vampire Apostles book 1)

A Dark Urban Vampire Romance

Release Date: 2021

SYNOPSIS
Despite being financed by his talented transgender prostitutes, a gritty, crack-addicted pimp unwillingly accepts the help of a vampire in exchange for surrendering his body and crack infused blood to satisfy the vampires own dark addictions. He believes his existence is inconsequential, but Jesus has other plans.

THE UNTAMED KING (Tales of Earthenstone book 1)

Release Date: 2021

SYNOPSIS *Earthenstone*
Amaron VelKoina: The rugged and bold specimen accidently killed a peer with one punch to the heart. He prospered in fighting arts, hunting, problem-solving, and the broad sword. Both feared and desired. As a young man in waiting, he had been kept chaste from women and prepared for becoming a King to a powerful Queen.

Queens of the Realm waited impatiently for him to be presented. Finally, after five years past due, he was formally presented to high society, pronouncing him as a young man ready for marriage. Close to his deaf mother, she let him procrastinate on marriage until enough was enough. Quickly enough, after formal courtship, his mother chose a perfect fit for her beloved eldest son, Queen Xerah IV of Earthenstone.

As Xerah's first husband, he had given her sons and none of the daughters she needed as heirs. It was common for Queens to take multiple husbands, so when Xerah took three more, after their years of marriage, Amaron bit his tongue and held his head high.

Yet, there was something strange about one of the new men in the palace. He was hiding something under those delicate features and soft voice. What sort of man was not excited about becoming a King? Xerah must have chosen him for his kitchen mastery and nothing more; it was obvious he was of the more...delicate and gentle type of men, not good for much else, like the breeding of daughters. He failed miserably at trying not to stare at Amaron's chiseled body. This was amusing. Could prove quite interesting considering Amaron was not a novice at initiating carnal attention from other men. Yet when Floran was not staring, he seemed dejected, paranoid and lost in thought.

Floran, had no choice: Run away or leave her mourning and vulnerable father. She couldn't leave him. Ever. Instead, she dressed as a young man to evade creditors until she could earn her way out of her family's debt. Life took a dangerous turn when she was meticulously chosen for her kitchen mastery skills as one of the three new husbands of Queen Xerah IV of Earthenstone.

Can Floran keep her identity a secret forever or tell it without being killed for deceiving the entire realm? Only when secrets are revealed and love distorts logic can Amaron fulfill his destiny.

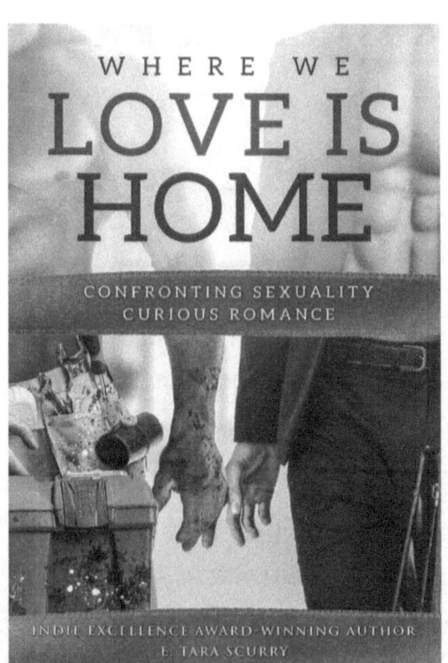

WHERE WE LOVE IS HOME

Release Date: 2022

Confronting Sexuality. Curious Romance

SYNOPSIS

A Latino general contractor and young American lawyer build an unlikely friendship that threatens their sexuality, destroys the status quo, and ignites their most deeply held desires.

HELL'S LOVER

Release Date: 2022

A blasphemous Book of Love. War. Forgiveness. Peace

SYNOPSIS

When an Archangel's world is literally turned upside down after following his abusive lover into Hell during The Rebellion, his lover's true soul mate, Lucifer, is consumed with fulfilling his destiny to annihilate every flicker of God's overwhelming power and love.

ANGELS WEAR ORCHIDS:

A Compilation of Poetry and Short Stories

Release Date: 2022

SYNOPSIS

Diverse and eccentric, Angels Wear Orchids is the second compilation of poetry and stories from award-winning author, E. Tara Scurry.

Beginning with the authors trademark distinctive prose, the first section of the book includes song lyrics and poetry. The second part includes five stories.

"The Cleaning Lady" follows a Vietnamese immigrant baited into a human trafficking ring when she arrives to interview as a housekeeper. She uses her creativity and courage to stay alive and plan her escape.

In "Three Leaf Clover" a workaholic black woman allows the two men she's dating to care for her cats when her boss unexpectedly sends her out of the country for work. Leery and resentful of each other, they eventually find more satisfying things to do with each other than share pet-sitting duties. When tragedy strikes this devoted threesome, a silver lining emerges.

"Pimp My Wheelchair" is a no holds barred dark comedy. It features a conceited wheelchair bound senior citizen and his clique of elderly and disabled friends who terrorize the patrons of Union Station in Washington DC.

"Tomorrow We Die" follows two comrades in arms as they make the most of their lives before facing one more excruciating battle against an opposing army.

In the title story "Angels Wear Orchids", the lead singer of a Neo-goth rock band falls in love with his sassy and hardworking personal assistant, to everyone's dismay, including hers. Being an interracial couple is the least of their differences: he's into scandalous erotic bondage and she wants nothing to do with it. He wants all of her attention and she needs to take care of family who sacrificed everything to support her success. She believes in what's Right and he believes in Right Now. Is their relationship worth the effort? Will their feelings leave them no choice but to give in to each other, despite the odds?

ABOUT THE AUTHOR

E. Tara Scurry lives her life's purpose by storytelling to make the world a better place and give reprieve and joy to those who need it most. You'll find her speaking at events and socializing on <u>Twitter</u>. Irrespective of creating in different genre's, her poetry and stories are always provoking, eccentric, inclusive, and openhearted. She writes about love, social problems, self-introspection, and the divine – all from a sociological perspective. She has gratefully added joy and thought-provoking experiences to her readers for over 3 decades; most of which was before she was formally published.

As a <u>Speaker</u>, she has taught at progressive places of worship, conferences, academic classes, and served as an inspirational speaker at Women's Retreats.

As a <u>Storyteller</u>, she believes her stories impact the world by making it more welcoming and inclusive. That the world is a better place when all feel safe, respected, and comfortable expressing all aspects of our identities. She believes that a whole life can change by one story. One experience can change a heart.

E. Tara Scurry is a graduate of Sweet Briar College and Johns Hopkins University's Carey Business School with a B.A in Sociology, Law & Society minor and a M.S. in Organizational Development & Strategic Human Resources.

A native of the D.C. Metropolitan area, she lives in Silver Spring, Maryland. Subscribe to her blog at https://etarascurry.com/blog/, and connect with her on Goodreads, Twitter https://twitter.com/etarascurry, Facebook, and YouTube.